Zilya's Secret Plan

ULRICH SCHAFFER
Illustrated by TAKASHI SHOJI

Lion Publishing

This is Zilya. She lives in a beautiful valley. There are green meadows in the valley, and tall trees. There are flowers and butterflies—and a river as blue as the sky. All around the valley are high mountains. There is snow on the mountains all the year round. When God made the world, Zilya thought, he must have wanted to make this valley especially beautiful.

Zilya likes to build little boats and float them down the river. She loves her beautiful valley very much.

One day, when she was watching her boats, she saw some people by the river. They were throwing all their empty bottles and cans into the water. Then they got into their car and started off in a rush. The wheels spun, crushing and chewing up the grass.

'Poor, poor grass!' said Zilya, stroking it gently. She was very sad to see the meadow grass hurt.

A few days later, more people came. They carved their names into the bark of a white birch. They laughed as they cut the tree—and did not hear the white birch scream. But Zilya heard.

'Little birch, don't cry, don't cry,' she said when the people had gone. 'Your bark will heal.' As soon as the birch heard Zilya's voice it stopped shivering and began to feel better.

Next day, Zilya saw a family having a picnic in the woods near her house. The children had slings. They shot at the trees, at the flowers, at the insects. A big, blue-black raven flew over their heads. They shot at that, and killed it. The raven dropped to the ground. The children just laughed and went on playing. Zilya couldn't believe her eyes. How could they?

Something had to be done.

Zilya went to the mayor of the village.

'People are spoiling our grass, hurting our trees and killing our creatures,' she said.

But the mayor wasn't listening. 'Go away, little girl,' he said. 'Can't you see I'm busy?'

The months went by, and many things happened in the valley to make Zilya sad.

'If this goes on, our beautiful valley will be spoiled,' she said to herself. And that was when she thought of her secret plan.

She called her friends to the place where the river and the forest and the meadow all meet. The animals gathered round. The blades of grass bent forward. No one wanted to miss a word that Zilya said. Even the birds stopped chirping. And the rabbits pricked up their long ears.

Zilya told them her plan.

Next morning the people in the village got up, and
looked out of their windows as usual. Strange. How
quiet it was! They couldn't hear any birds.
    'Where have all the birds gone? What's happening?'
Zilya knew what was happening.
She had planned it. But she didn't say a word.

The day after that, all the animals were gone.
   No squirrels were gathering food.
   No rabbits hopped across the meadows.
   There were no moles, no mice, no foxes, no badgers—
anywhere.

On the third day all the insects had disappeared.
  No buzzing flies.
  No bugs, no beetles, no bees, no wasps.
  No grasshoppers whirred in the meadow.
  No butterflies fluttered from flower to flower.
  No ants scurried to and fro.
And in the evening, no moths gathered around the light.

On the fourth day there was an even bigger surprise. When the people in the village looked out of their windows, there were no trees.

The poplars around the school were gone.

The big oak tree in the middle of the village, where the children loved to play, had disappeared.

So had the birches and willows, the maples and beeches.

Even the fir-trees on the mountains had gone.

The valley looked empty and bare.

That evening there was a meeting in the village. 'What's happening?' everyone asked. 'First the birds, then the animals and the insects – and now all the trees. Where have they gone? What *is* happening?'

The people were shouting by now. But no one knew the answer. They asked the mayor, but he didn't know, either.

Zilya was there. But when she tried to speak the grown-ups said, 'What are you doing here? This isn't a meeting for children.' And they sent her home.

On the fifth day the grass was gone. One of the people, who got up early, saw the last blades of grass disappearing. Only the bare earth remained, brown and black.

The cows walked around in surprise: there was nothing for them to eat.

Another meeting was called. Once again, Zilya went. This time she stepped right up to the mayor.

'Mr Mayor, I know what we must do.' But again he refused to listen.

'You here again?' he said – and rudely pushed her aside.

'If you don't listen,' Zilya called to him, 'something worse will happen tomorrow!' Then she put her hands behind her back and walked away. She didn't even turn round.

Next day, it was true, something worse *had* happened.

The river was empty.

There was no water for the cows, or the people, to drink.

Everyone could see the ugly, rusty tins and rubbish sticking out of the mud at the bottom of the river.

At midday the sun was hot and the river began to smell. It seemed as if the whole valley was dying.

Now the valley was really dead. Everything was drab and grey. Sadly the people thought about their beautiful valley.

Someone said: 'It seems as if God is taking back all the lovely things he made and gave us.'

At last the people began to understand how much they needed the birds, the animals, the insects, the trees, the grass—and the sparkling, rushing, singing river.

When the mayor saw the dried-up river he remembered
what Zilya had said.

'Zilya,' he said, 'tell me how you knew that
something worse would happen.'

'It was all part of the plan,' Zilya said. And she
told the mayor the whole story. She told him how the
creatures of the valley were afraid, because no one
took care of them. She told him how they had planned
to leave, to show people just what the valley would be
like without them.

Then the mayor called the village people together.

'We have to take better care of our valley,' he said.
'When God made the world, he put us in charge of it.
He told us to take care of all his creatures. But we
haven't done it. Zilya has shown us what our valley
is like without all these things. We have to change.
From now on, all the rubbish must be tidied up and
taken away. We must protect the flowers and the
animals. Anyone who hurts them will be punished.
And no one is allowed to cut down trees without
special permission.'

He said a lot of other things, too. Then he turned to
Zilya: 'Please tell all your friends to come back now.
We love them and we promise to take better care of
them.'

Zilya knew he really meant it. She was very happy.

Next morning Zilya packed a knapsack and set off into the mountains where all her friends were hiding.

When they saw her they came out to meet her.

'You can all come back again,' she said. 'The plan has worked. The people have changed. They have remembered how God told them to take care of you. They know they can't live without you.'

When they heard this they were all very happy, for they knew they belonged to the valley. They began to move down the hillside, towards the village.

The birds flew overhead, singing their very best songs.

The river began to flow again, and the fish leaped.

The rabbits and the foxes and all the other animals hopped and skipped and jumped in the air for joy.

The green grass grew again in the valley.

The trees marched like an army. As the wind rushed through their branches, Zilya could hear the happy chatter of the leaves.

Right across the village street was a banner: WELCOME HOME! The village had its best party ever. Everyone joined in, but Zilya was the most important guest. Zilya had saved the valley, and everyone knew it.

WELCOME HOME!

Lion Publishing
121 High Street, Berkhamsted, Herts, England

Copyright © 1978 Oncken Verlag, Wuppertal, Germany

First English language edition 1978

ISBN 0 85648 086 X

Printed in Germany